ISOLA™

2
BRENDEN FLETCHER / KARL KERSCHL
STORY
KARL KERSCHL / MSASSYK
ART
ADITYA BIDIKAR
LETTERS
image

Production assistance by Ryan Brewer

ISOLA, VOL. 2. First Printing. July 2020. Published by Image Comics, Inc. Office of publication: 2701 NW Vaughn St., Suite 780, Portland, OR 97210. Printed in the USA. Representation: Law Offices of Harris M. Miller II, P.C (right.inquiries@gmail.com). ISBN: 978-1-5343-1353-8.

High blood cleft twain
'fore time's false plea
Pestilent root
Of the hollow tree

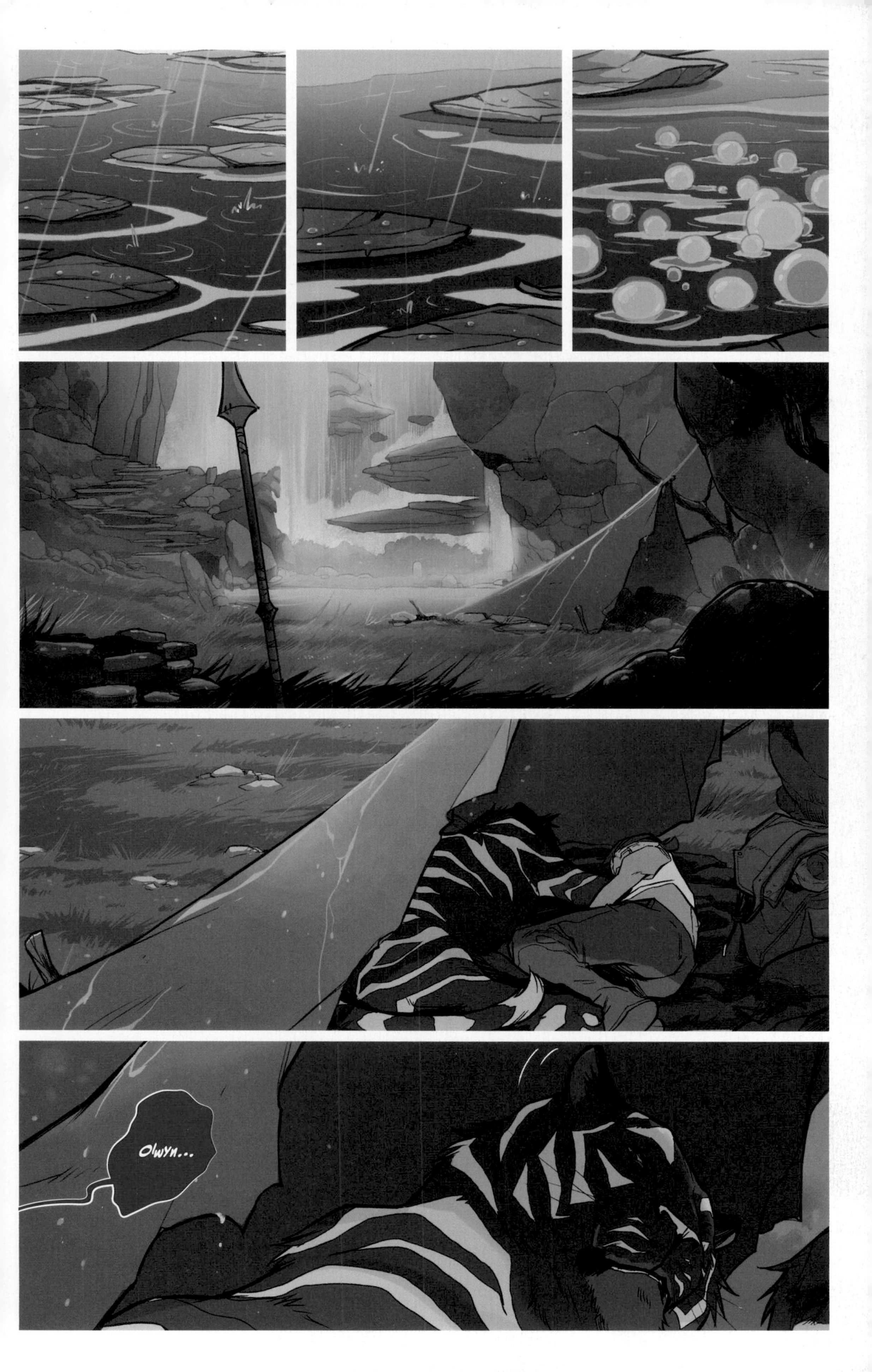
Olwyn...

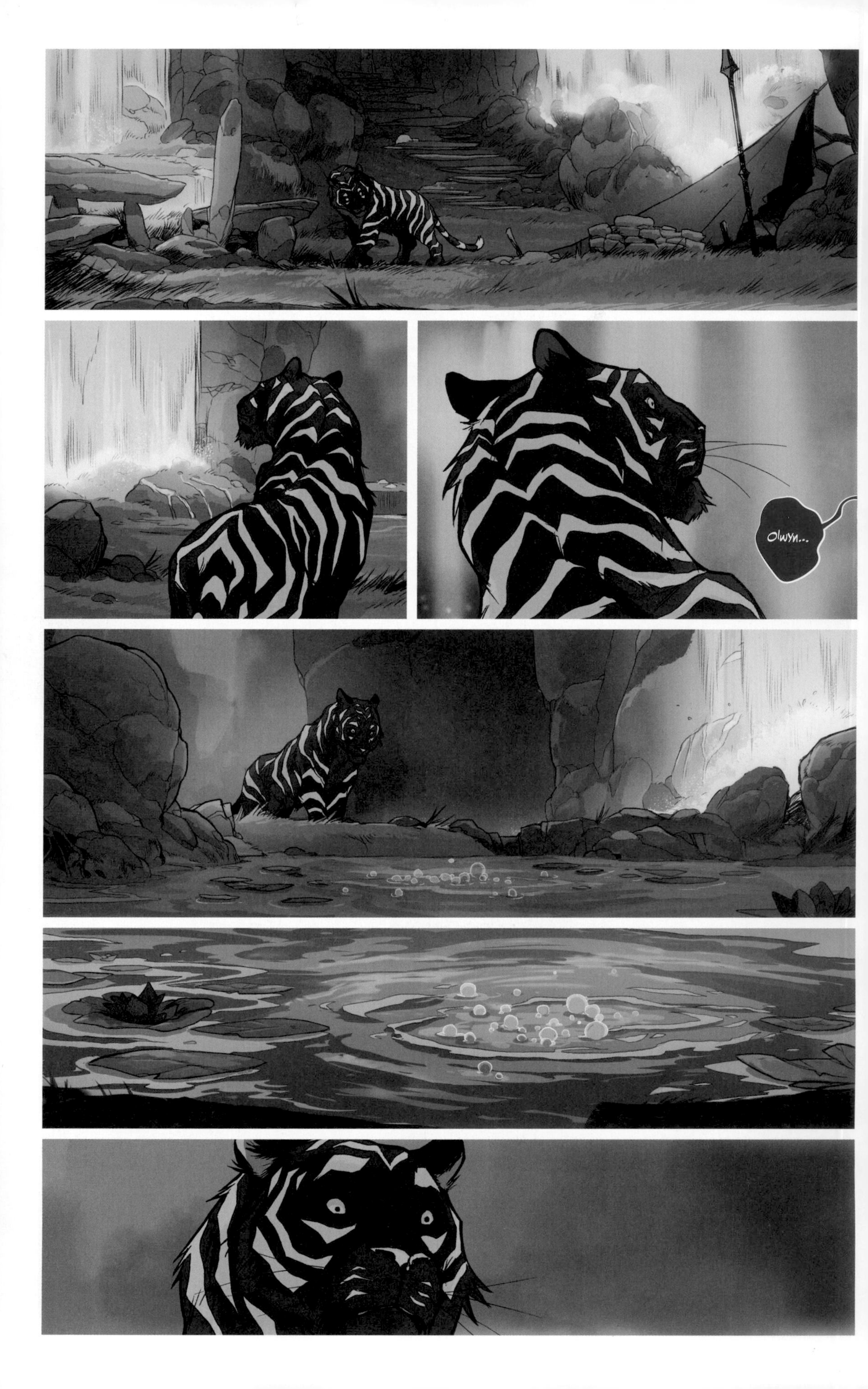
Olwyn...

little one...

MOTHER?
HELP... ME...
MOTHER!

unf...
ASHER!!
ASHER, HELP!!
HAHH...
hahh... I--I'VE GOT YOU.
ASHER AND FATHER WILL--
Olwyn... please...
Take me baaaack...

Take me...
baaaaaaaack...

CKAAA
CKAAAAAAA
CKAAAA
CKAAAAAAA

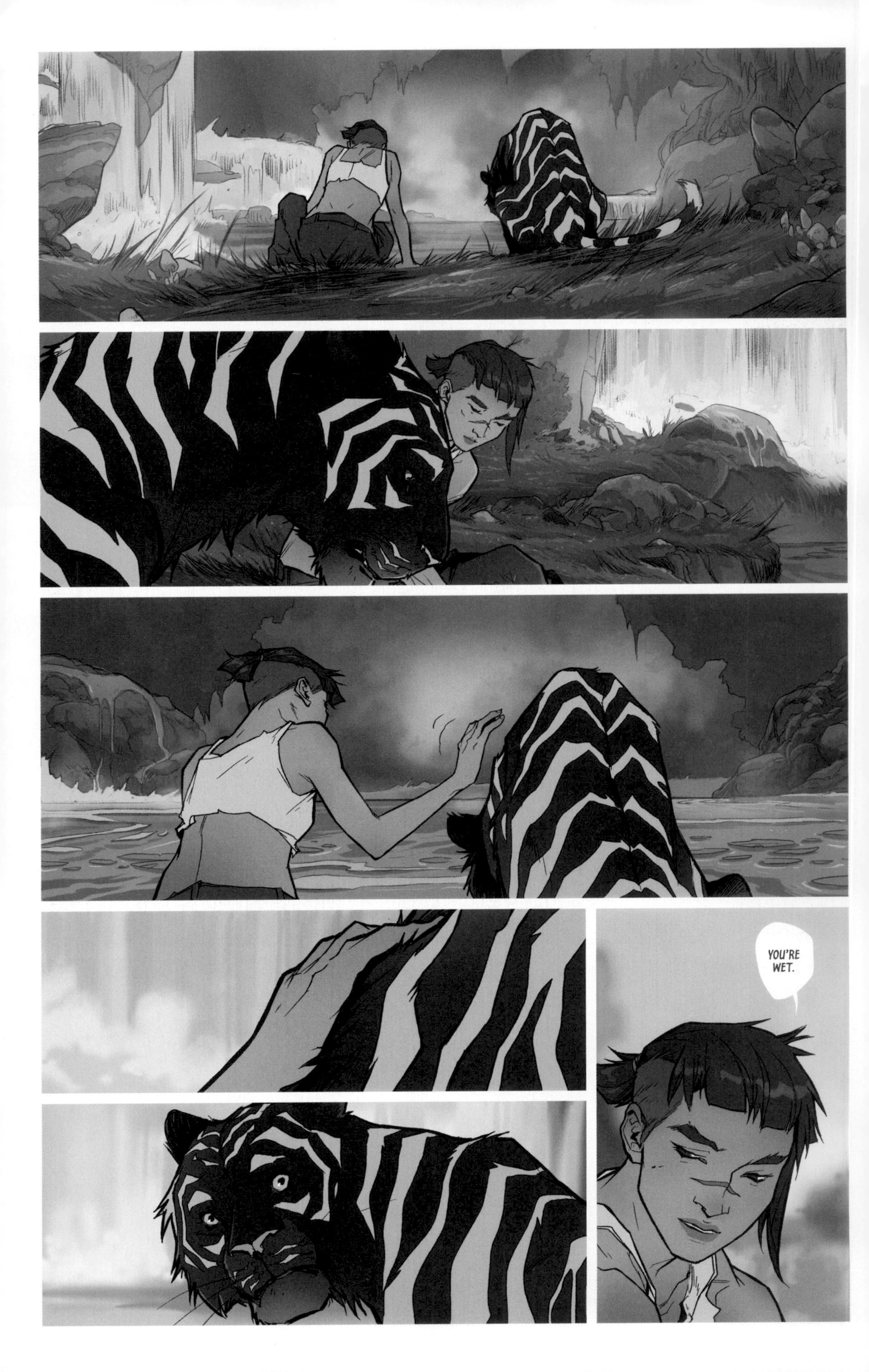
YOU'RE WET.

I'LL START SOME BREAKFAST.
YOU'RE OKAY, RIGHT?

SUN'S COMING UP.

I KNOW WHAT YOU SAID YOU SAW BUT...
IF THE GHOST WOOD'S NEAR ISOLA THERE'S NOTHING ABOUT IT IN HERE.

UNLESS THIS IS SUPPOSED TO BE--

HEY!

WE'RE NOT ALONE OUT HERE.
HOLD TIGHT.

IT *IS* ONE OF OURS. FREK.
BUT ALSO, THANK THE GODS. THIS IS A GIFT. THEY'LL HAVE EVERY-THING WE NEED.

I SHOULD BE ABLE TO BLEND IN AND MAKE MY WAY TO THE SUPPLY TENT.

MOST OF OUR TROOPS WILL BE WELL INTO THEIR RATIONS BY THIS TIME OF THE MORNING.

IF THEY'RE FOCUSED ON THEIR PLATES, THEY WON'T BE LOOKING AT MY FACE.

WISH ME LUCK.

...opening ourselves up for attack, if you ask me.
Out in the open like this? The Hallum can just--

YVAN DON'T FRET NO HALLUM.
Mmf--
GO ON YOUR WHINING.

...pulls her own skin right off over her head, swear to gods.
Go on.

Never seen anything like it.

YOU, WITH THE VISOR!

YEAH, YOU!

LOOKIN' OUTTA PLACE THERE, SOLDIER.
YOU'RE THE ONLY ONE WITHOUT A CUPPA JANNY'S BREW.
GOOD, RIGHT?
SSA

AHA!
GULF of LEGENDRE
Mmm!
C-CAPTAIN ROOK...?

THEY SAID YOU K-KILLED THE PRINCE AND--
shh!
TELL ME YOUR NAME, SQUIRE.
ROBIRD, SIR.
ROBIRD, CAN I TRUST YOU?
Y-YES, SIR.

NO ONE CAN KNOW I'M HERE.
I'M ON A SECRET MISSION TO SAVE OUR QUEEN FROM AN EVIL ENCHANTMENT AND I NEED THESE SUPPLIES TO HELP HER MAKE THE JOURNEY.
BUT, SIR, THEY--

THEY SAID QUEEN OLWYN WERE KIDNAPPED. MAYBE KILLED.
WE'S ON OUR WAY TO PALAGRINE ROCK TO--

THE QUEEN IS ALIVE, ROBIRD. SHE'LL BE BACK HOME IN MAAR VERY SOON. SHE'S PUTTING HER FAITH IN ALL HER PEOPLE WHILE SHE'S AWAY, TO STAY AT HOME, PROTECT HER BORDERS. SHE--

WHAT KIND OF ENCHANTMENT?

WHAT DO YOU MEAN?

WHAT HAPPENED TO QUEEN, THEN?
WERE IT A WITCH?

YOU CAN'T TELL ANYONE. NOT THE KNIGHT YOU SERVE, NOT EVEN THE WIND.
GOT IT?

ON THE LIFE O' THE QUEEN, ON THE BLOOD O' MY MOTHERS, SIR.

IF WE CAN CROSS HERE, WE AVOID OUR SCOUTING PARTY COMPLETELY.
AND WE STEER CLEAR OF PALAGRINE ROCK.

RIVER'S NOT MUCH FURTHER ON AND BEYOND THAT, OLD KINGSLAND...
THERE'S NO OTHER WAY TO GET TO THE GHOSTWOOD.

LET'S SPLIT UP AND LOOK FOR A PATH.

IT'S A LONG WAY DOWN...

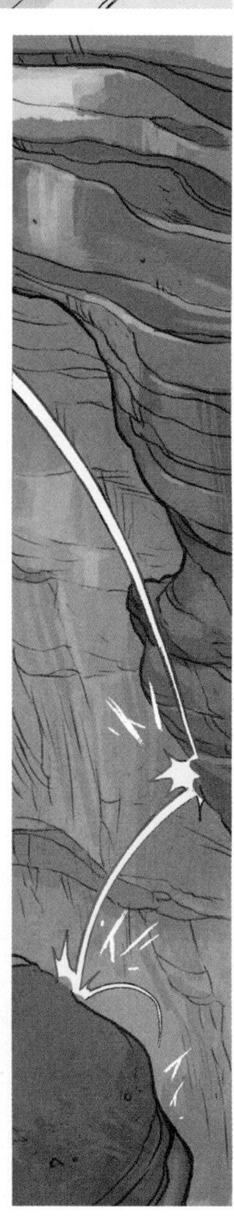

IT'S AN OLD QUARRY LIFT, I THINK.
RUSTED PRETTY TIGHT.

YEAH. I'M NOT LETTING YOU ON THIS THING.
NOT SURE I TRUST THESE STAIRS, EITHER.

YOUR MAJESTY, I WOULDN'T--

OKAY.

Kaji...
WE INVOKE YOUR NAME AND FOLLOW YOUR STEPS... TO GUIDE US THROUGH THESE LANDS.
LOST IS FOUND AND FOUND IS SOUND... IN THE CRADLE OF YOUR HANDS.
WE HAVE NO KOMA BRANCHES AS OFFERING...
BUT PLEASE PROTECT US ON OUR TRAVELS.

AAAAAAH
NO! NO! NOOOOO!!
!!

NNAAAAAHHH
huhh
a-huhhhh

WH-- WHAT...?
LEAVE HER BE.

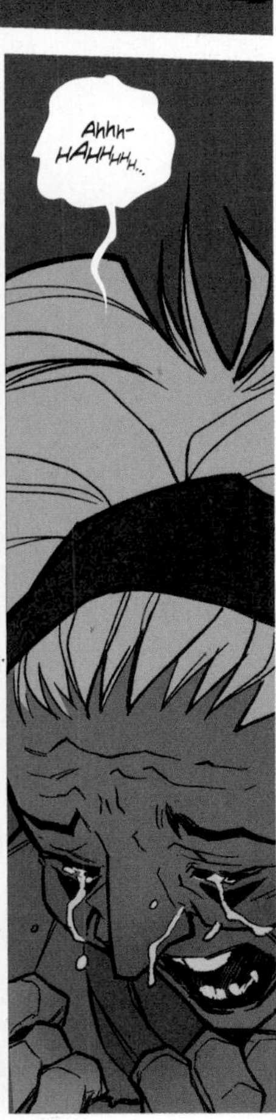
Ahhh- HAHHHHH...

BROKEN VESSEL, BROKEN CHILD.
YOSHIA'S DAUGHTER WON'T BE COMING BACK IN THIS LIFE.

SHE'S IN KAJI'S CARE. LIKE THE REST OF OUR LITTLES.

I--I'M SO SORRY...
T'--NO WAY YOU COULD KNOW, SOLDIER. YOU'RE NAUGHT BUT A BREATH O' FATE BLOWING INTO OUR VILLAGE. IF IT HADN'T BEEN YOU, IT'D BE SOMETHING ELSE.
WHEN A THING'S MEANT TO BE, IT'S MEANT TO BE.

AND THIS...? YOUR CHILD?
MORO HAVE DONE UNSPEAKABLE THINGS TO OUR CHILDREN AS WELL.

WHAT? NO. SHE'S, UH...
THE TIGER IS MY COMPANION. SHE'S PERFECTLY, UM, TAME.

SHE'S AN OLD SOUL, THIS ONE.

IT'S LATE. YOU TWO COME INSIDE.
THERE'S FOOD AND WARMTH.

YOU'RE COME FROM MAAR?
UH, JUST OUTSIDE, IN THE COUNTRY. MY FATHER WAS A FARMER.
I USED TO WORK IN THE CAPITAL BUT...I LEFT TO FIND OTHER WORK.
OH. SAW YOUR ARMOUR AND THOUGHT MAYBE YOU WERE HERE TO ASK ON ABOUT THE NEXT SHALE SHIPMENT. WON'T BE OUT YOUR WAY FOR A WHILE, I'M AFRAID.

NOT MANY STRONG FOLK LEFT TO WORK THE QUARRY SINCE PALAGRINE ROCK CAME CALLING.
BLOODY BASTIAN BUILDING HIS ARMY...

TO KEEP THE DARK ONES OUT. IF YOU'RE OF THIS WORLD, YOU'LL CROSS FREELY.

MORO WOULD STEAL AWAY YOUNG 'UNS WHO DIDN'T BEHAVE.
I'M SURE YOUR OWN MA WARNED YOU SAME-LIKE WHEN YOU WERE WEE...

PEOPLE OF THE MIST WILL SNATCH YOU UP IF YOU HURT YOUR LITTLE SISTER OR TALK BACK TO YOUR PARENTS OR WHATNOT.
AND MAYBE IT HAPPENED ONCE, YEARS BACK. MAYBE A CHILD *DID* GO MISSING. I DON'T RECALL.
BUT IT WAN'T LONG AGO THINGS STARTED TO CHANGE.

FIRST ONE. THEN ANOTHER. AND THEN THE WHOLE LOT OF 'EM. ALL GONE.
...thank you.

NOT A ONE.

WAIT... THERE ARE NO CHILDREN LEFT HERE? NONE AT ALL?

THEY COME ALL THE WAY DOWN THE QUARRY? THE MORO?

SHALE GOES MISSING. SOMETIMES FOOD. THERE'S PAW PRINTS AROUND.
THAT'S ALL USED TO HAPPEN, UNTIL...

THIS IS MINE. TAKEN THREE YEARS AGO, BUT I NEVER LOSE HOPE.
KAJI-NAM KAJI.

THIS WAS HERS. THE FIRST TO GO.

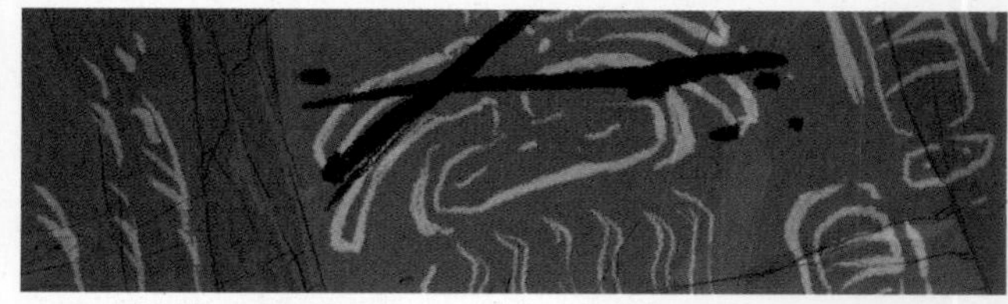

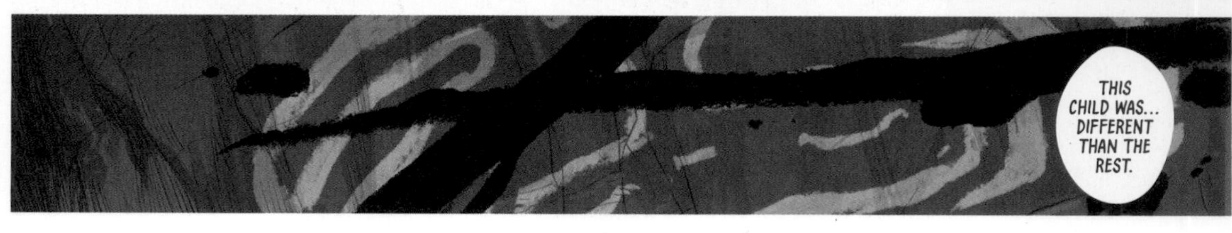
THIS CHILD WAS... DIFFERENT THAN THE REST.

SMELL JUST LIKE HER. THE TWO OF YEH.

DIRT SPIRITS. MAGICKS.
I'LL NOT BE HAVIN' IT BACK HERE. IF YEH KNOW WHAT'S GOOD FOR YEH, YEH'LL CLEAR THE FREK OFF THIS NIGHT.
NO PLACE DOWN HERE FOR YEH.

AN' IF THAT'S A TIGER I'VE GOT TWO GOOD EYES.

LADY, I DON'T KNOW WHAT YOU'RE ABOUT BUT WE'RE TIRED. WE JUST WANT--
YEH SEE HER, YEH TELL HER THERE'S NO HOME FOR HER HERE. NOT NOW OR EVER.

GHOST, HO!!

GHOST, HO!!
WE GOT ONE!
CAUGHT PULLING TROUT ON THE WETLAND BORDER.

WAIT!
WAIT!
IS THAT LAMM? I THINK IT COULD BE!

TOO SOON TO TELL. S'ALL FUR.
IT IS HIM!

LAMM? IS THAT YOU? DO YOU REMEMBER?
DID YOU COME HOME TO ME, BOY?

LOOSEN HIS CHAINS, GUSS! HE CAN'T BREATHE!

DON'T YOU DARE.
IT'S TOO SOON.

COME ON, NOW.
WE'D BEST PERFORM THE RITES TO KNOW FOR SURE.

IF IT LIVES FOR ONE FULL PHASE OF THE MOON, KAJI WILL REVEAL IT TO BE ONE OF OUR CHILDREN. IF NOT...
LIFT THE BOY, GUSS.

'TIS DONE, CHILD.
COME AWAY WITH US NOW AND LET THE SPIRIT GET TO ITS WORK.

I KNOW.
BUT I'M NOT SURE WE SHOULD GET INVOLVED HERE. FOR ALL WE KNOW THE MORO *DID* DO THIS.
I JUST THINK...OUR OBJECTIVE IS TO GET TO ISOLA.

BUT IF YOU COMMAND ME TO UNTIE IT, I WILL, YOUR MAJESTY...

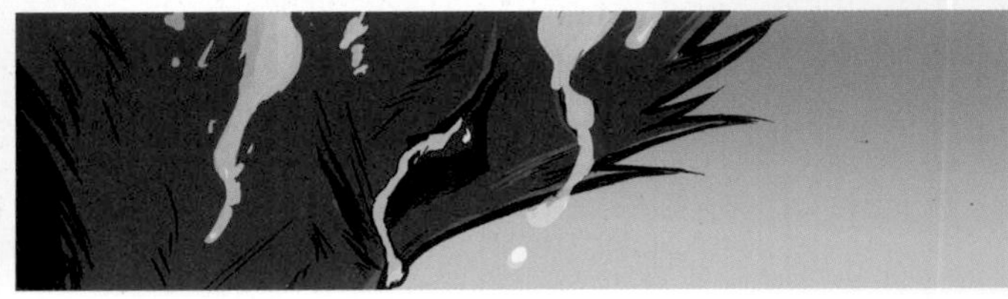

snrk

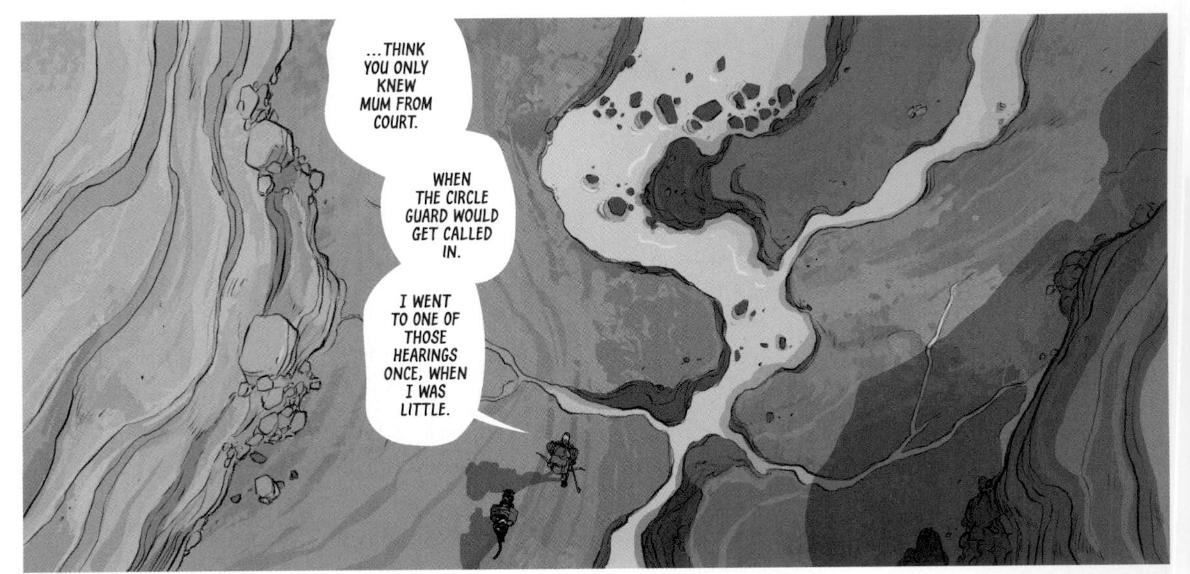
...THINK YOU ONLY KNEW MUM FROM COURT.
WHEN THE CIRCLE GUARD WOULD GET CALLED IN.
I WENT TO ONE OF THOSE HEARINGS ONCE, WHEN I WAS LITTLE.

I GUESS THIS IS ALL RUN-OFF FROM THE LEGENDRE?
IT MUST HAVE FLOWED THROUGH THIS WHOLE CANYON BEFORE IT WAS DAMMED UP FOR MINING.
hup!

WE DID THE RIGHT THING, COMING THIS WAY.
WE'RE PROTECTED DOWN HERE AND THE ARMY WILL HAVE TAKEN THE BOLTHO PASS TOWARD THE COAST.

Ah, HERE WE GO.

ALL RIGHT, SO WE'RE HERE. AND THE RIVER IS JUST ON THE OTHER SIDE.
WE SHOULD BE ABLE TO FOLLOW IT WESTWARD UNTIL THE NARROWS AND CROSS THERE, BEFORE COPHONY.
!

!!

WHAT THE GODS ARE THEY ON ABOUT?

stop...

I...I c-can't...

...hnf
HUFF.

Ouch. Too steep. I can't pay that.
That's price. Take it or no.

OH, *THAT'S PRICE?*
SO MAYBE I SHOULD BUY FROM DUTCH BOWS, THEN? *THEY* TREAT ME RIGHT. NO HAGGLING. NO CHEAP CUTS...
AND THEY *SMELL* A LOT BETTER THAN--
GRAMBLEGAW CLAN SMELLS BEST. IS BEST DEAL. TAKE OR NO.

FINE. JUST GIVE IT TO ME.
I'm paying you in *soap* next time...

help...

help us...

Who is awake, and who is asleep...
Oh, you're okay, sweetie. You're okay.

KITTY KITTY KITTY.
YOUR SWEETIE HAS A FEVER.
I HAVE MEDICINE AT MY PLACE, AND THE SOFTEST BED.

AREN'T YOU TWO JUST THE SORRIEST COUPLE.
YOU'RE *SO* LUCKY YOU FOUND ME.

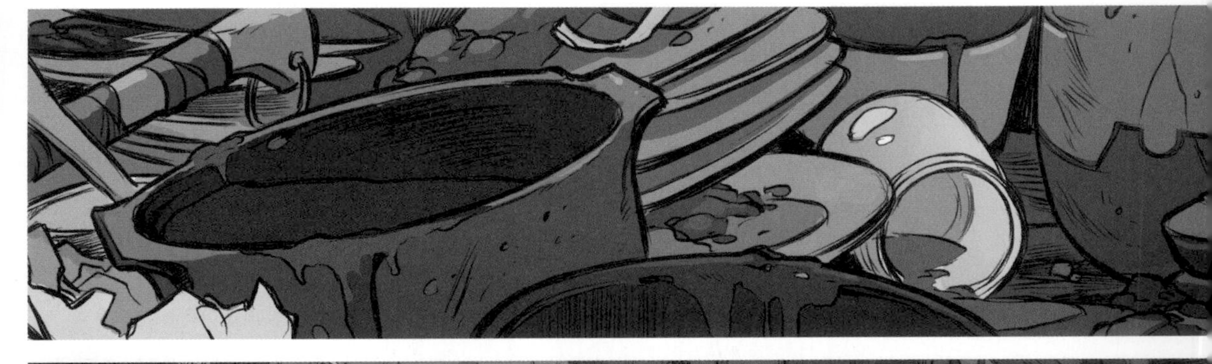

LOOK AT YOUR BEAUTIFUL FACE.
WHAT HAPPENED TO YOU, SWEETIE? WHO DID THIS?

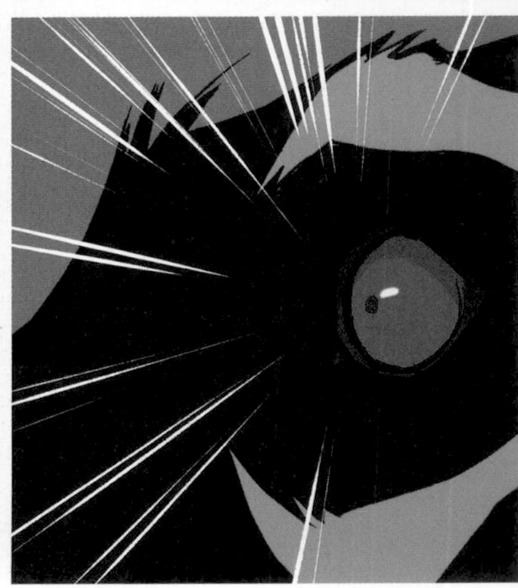

FEELS LIKE... MMM...
SOMETHING DARK.
AND TERRIBLE.
HEY!
MINE.

...hm mmm hm

...bound with vines

...hm hm mmm

...by the stars in the sky... You'll be mine...

YOU'LL BE MINE... YOU'LL BE--

MORNING, TIGER.
SLEEP WELL?

...Olwyn?

Unf... WHOSE BED IS THIS? HOW--?
OH, THANK THE NIGHT, YOU'RE UP...

LET ME SEE YOU...
OLWYN?
LOOK HERE. LOOK AT ME.
OH, BABY, YOU'RE DOING JUST...JUST PERFECT.

YOU'RE GOING TO BE FINE.

I THINK YOUR FRIEND LOOKED INTO THE EYE OF THE HALLUM, KITTY.
THEY REACH INTO YOUR HEAD AND MIX ALL THE GOOD STUFF AROUND.

PLEASE...
WHO ARE YOU?
A FRIEND.
EVERYONE NEEDS FRIENDS. AND NOW YOU'VE GOT ME.

YOU CAN CALL ME MILUŠE.
YOU'RE WELCOME TO MY BED AS LONG AS YOU NEED IT, HONEY. YOU REALLY SHOULDN'T GO ANYWHERE IN YOUR CONDITION.
YOU NEED YOUR MEDICINE.

AH, *STICKS.*
I'LL HAVE TO MAKE ANOTHER POT.

HERE, JUST GET THIS IN YOU FOR NOW AND I'LL--
THANK YOU BUT... OW...
WE NEED TO GET BACK ON THE ROAD.

IT'S JUST A LITTLE SIP, SWEETIE.
DRINK...

DRINK...

Whoa...
I DON'T KNOW WHAT--

YOU'RE SAFE HERE.
DRINK THIS UP...

...AND YOU'LL BE BETTER IN NO TIME.

...hm
hm
mmm

...YOU'RE REALLY THE MOST UNGRATEFUL LITTLE SNIG, LUKAZ.
YOU AND YOUR BIG SISTER.

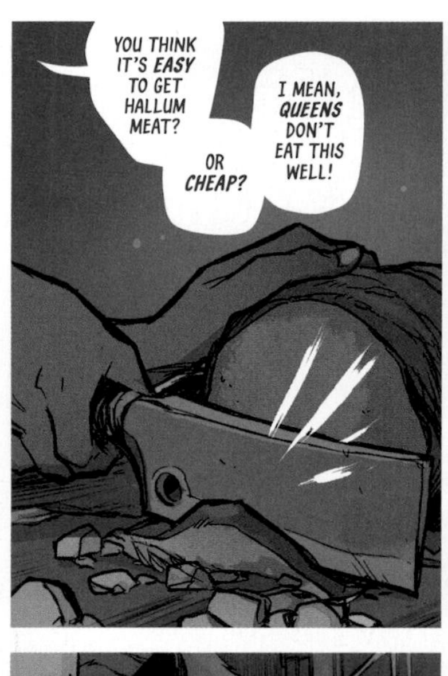
YOU THINK IT'S EASY TO GET HALLUM MEAT?
OR CHEAP?
I MEAN, QUEENS DON'T EAT THIS WELL!

BUT WE HAVE A SPECIAL GUEST NOW, DON'T WE? AND IF WE WANT HER TO FEEL AT HOME WE CAN'T SPARE ANY EXPENSE.

NOW THE SECRET INGREDIENT...

OW!

DO YOU KNOW WHAT I COULD DO TO YOU?!

NEXT TIME, I'LL GRIND YOU INTO THE BREW, LUKAZ.
FIRST ONE LITTLE TOE, THEN ANOTHER LITTLE TOE, UNTIL ALL THE LITTLE TOES ARE GONE.
THAT GOES FOR THE REST OF YOU, TOO.

Mmm.

...MM!
MMMM!

Mm.
THIS IS JUST... JUST THE BEST. HAVING YOU HERE.
I'VE WAITED SO LONG.

I DON'T WANT YOU TO EVER EVER LEAVE.

OH!
HEY! WHAT'S THAT ALL ABOUT?
WE'RE GUESTS HERE!

OH, THANK YOU. I WAS SO FRIGHTENED.
WILD BEASTS HAVE NO PLACE IN A HAPPY HOME.

I AGREE.

Hmm hm hm
AND FREE FROM MOORS THE CASTLE FLED TO DANCE AMONG THE CLOUDS SO TRUE MY LOVE WOULD BE
SO TRUE MY LOVE WOULD BE Hmm hm hm
Hm...? ME?
IS THAT ME?
MAYBE?
MAYBE I'LL LET YOU BE MY HOME.
I DON'T KNOW WHAT THAT MEANS BUT IT SOUNDS... NICE.

WE HAD MALINES AT HOME BUT DAD NEVER GREW THEM THIS BIG.
YOU WERE FARMERS?
DAD WAS.
I DIDN'T HAVE THE TOUCH.
MMM...
CAN I?
OF COURSE, LOVE.

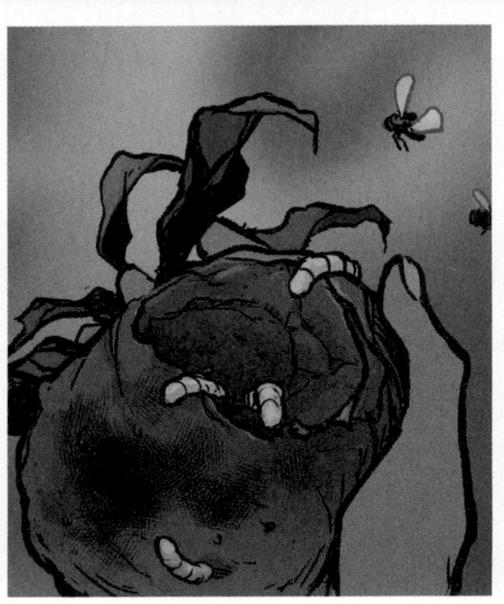

...ngf?

Ugh!
PTTOO!
IT'S ROTTEN.
THEY'RE ALL...IT'S ALL ROTTEN.
OH NO, HONEY, NO.
I THINK YOU'VE STILL GOT A TOUCH OF SICKNESS.

WAIT...
Olwyn?
YOU'RE BURNING UP, LOVE.

LET'S GET YOU BACK TO BED.
GET SOME MORE HOT COFFEE INTO YOU.

HAW!
HAW!

HAW!

HAW!

HAW!
HAW!
HA—

help!
help us!
please!
help us!
... help

help

help us

help

help

WHAT DID I TELL YOU DIRTY LITTLE SNIGS I WOULD DO TO--
...YOU.

BITCH!
hngk!

ung

hahh
D-DON'T COME ANY CLOSER.
I'M PROTECTED.

YOU'RE NOT WELCOME HERE.

TIME FER YEH TO COME HOME NOW, CHILD.

YE BEEN OUT IN THE WILD TOO LONG.
LOOK AT YEH...

Y-YOU TOLD ME TO LEAVE.
SAID I'D MAKE THE WHOLE QUARRY SICK.

THEY'VE FORGIVEN YEH. KAJI'S FORGIVEN YEH.
JUST COME ON OUT NOW.

YOU CALLED ME... UNHOLY.

BUT LOOK AT YEH NOW! MOMMA'S WEE GIRL AGAIN.
COME AND GEE' US A WEE HUG, CHILD...

I...
I'VE...

...GOT YOU!
EEEEEE

EEEE
EEEEE

EEEEEE--ehk
STOP STRUGGLING, COW.
YOU'RE JUST MAKING THE BINDING THAT MUCH STRONGER.
LET'S SEE HOW *YOU* LIKE BEING CHAINED UP, HUH?
HUH?
SEE IF *KAJI* THINKS YOU'RE WORTH SAVING.
YOU PRAY TO *ME* NOW.
...ngh
NO...
THE SPELL...

NO!
GODSDAMN LITTLE SNIGS! I NEED MORE--
JUST-- JUST NEED ONE MORE CUP OF BREW AND...
I'LL BE-- hnn... MYSELF.
...hngh
...hnngh
unholy.
...SHUT UP.
Unholy on the outside. Unholy inside.
I SAID SHUT UP!
EE EEEE EE

Mma...
ma...
MAMA
MAMA
MAMA

GHOST, HO!
KAJI BE PRAISED! ROUND 'EM UP AND GET 'EM BACK TO THE QUARRY.
CAN'T BE.

EASY. EASY NOW, GIRL.

BACK NOW, CAT. DON'T KNOW WHAT BUSINESS THIS IS OF YOURS...
...BUT THESE LITTLE ONES ARE SHALE FOLK OR I'LL BE LANCED.

ON NOW, KINDERS!
KAJI'LL HAVE THE TRUTH OUT OF YA.
KAJI-NAM KAJI. THE RITES REVEAL ALL TRUTHS.

MILUŠE?

...HELLO?
MILUŠE? WHERE...

Ngf

Olwyn?

OLWYN?
She'll never...love you...like thisss...
YOU!!
I TOLD YOU TO SHUT UP!

When she sees... what you've done...
...what you did... to those childrennnn...

What you did...to meeeeee

OLWYN?!

OLWYN!
...please.

FREK!
FREK.
FREK.
FREK.
I'VE GOT NO BUSINESS BEING A QUEEN'S GUARD.
YOU KNEW IT. THEY TOLD YOU.
YOU WANTED ME ANYWAY...
AND I FAILED YOU AND MAAR AND...
I'M JUST A BORDER GUARD.

CAPTAIN...

DON'T BE SO HARD ON YOURSELF.

OLWYN! YOU--
Shh...

AND FREE FROM
MOORS THE CASTLE FLED
TO DANCE AMONG THE CLOUDS
SO TRUE MY LOVE
WOULD BE

Hmm hm hm...

Mmm...

GOOD MORNING, MY LOVE.
MM--
MORNING?

YOU'RE STILL HERE.
ARE YOU STILL HERE? AM...AM I DREAMING? I DON'T KNOW WHAT'S REAL ANYMORE--

SHHH. IT'S NOT A DREAM.

WE CAN... WE CAN GO HOME.
BACK TO MAAR.
YOU'RE PARCHED, SWEETIE.

WE HAVE HOURS YET 'TIL DAYBREAK AND I'M NOT READY TO SHARE YOU WITH ANYONE.
HOME IS WHERE THE HEART IS, AFTER ALL.

OH, GODS...THE REGIMENT!
WE HAVE TO PULL THEM BACK.
IF OUR LADS MAKE IT TO PALAGRINE ROCK, IT'LL BE WAR!

THEY'LL HAVE CROSSED THE *SHALE* BY NOW.
I SAW THEIR ORDERS. IT'S A SOUTHERN ROUTE, TOWARD PENETANG.

FREK!
IF WE HURRY WE CAN HEAD THEM OFF.
ROOK...

ROOK...
I'VE WAITED SO LONG FOR THIS MOMENT.
LET'S AT LEAST TAKE THE MORNING. WE DESERVE IT.

WE'LL GO BACK TO THE HOUSE, FRESHEN UP, AND TALK ABOUT WHAT NEEDS TO BE DONE.
YOUR QUEEN IS BACK. NO ONE IS GOING TO DIE.

I PROMISE.

THAT'S MY GIRL.
I'M GOING TO MAKE YOU THE JUICIEST BREAKFAST. OF PLOVER'S EGGS AND MASHED GULOO. AND BERRIES!
DID YOU KNOW I CAN COOK?

I KNOW SO MANY THINGS! IT'S WONDERFUL. THINGS I NEVER KNEW THAT I KNEW.
OH, ONCE I'M BACK ON MY THRONE, ALL WILL BE RIGHT WITH THE WORLD. NO MORE WAR. NO MORE HUNTING...

THE TWO OF US TOGETHER.
NO MORE BACKSTABBING FAMILY TO TAKE EVERYTHING AWAY FROM US.

YOUR BROTHER WAS... TOUCHED, OLWYN.
I DON'T KNOW HOW HE CHANGED YOU BUT I CAN'T BELIEVE HE WAS--

I'M TALKING ABOUT MY BITCH OF A MOTHER!

MY MOTHER! NOT ASHER.
THAT TWIT DOESN'T HAVE A MALICIOUS BONE IN HIS BODY.
WE...WE PLAYED TOGETHER AS CHILDREN... DIDN'T WE?

I loved Queen Branwen.
SHE WAS ALWAYS KIND TO ME AND MY FAMILY IN COURT.

KIND?
MY MOTHER'S A **MONSTER,** ROOK.
YOU HAVE NO IDEA HOW SHE RUINS--HOW SHE **RUINED** LIVES.
SHE CAST ME OUT OF THE QUARRY WHEN I WAS BARELY OF AGE. OUT OF HER LIFE. FOR WHAT?

OLWYN.
YOU'RE NOT MAKING ANY SENSE.
...said I was sick. **SHE** was the sick one.
She was...the Queen...
YES, THE QUEEN.

I DON'T KNOW WHAT WENT ON INSIDE THE KINGDOM. FROM THE FARM IT SEEMED LIKE THE MOST MAGICAL PLACE.
BUT I KNOW THAT MOM WAS SO PROUD WHENEVER SHE RETURNED FROM DUTY. SERVING THE QUEEN AND MAAR WERE EVERYTHING TO HER.

She had your mother **KILLED,** Rook.
SHE MIGHT AS WELL HAVE SHOT THE ARROW HERSELF.

KNEEL, ROOK.
BY THE GODS, CHILD...

How... long...?
She was a coward and a liar. They ALL are...

HOW LONG HAVE YOU KNOWN SHE ORDERED THE DEATH OF MY MOTHER?

Hm?
I KNOW NOW.
I GUESS I'VE KNOWN FOR YEARS.
My head is so full...

AND YOU DIDN'T THINK TO TELL ME?
EVEN THOUGH WE...?

YAAH!

Pant... pant...

ROOK.

CAPTAIN ROOK.

AS YOUR QUEEN, WHAT I DO AND DO NOT CHOOSE TO TELL YOU IS MY CONCERN.
WE SHOULD BE THANKFUL THAT OUR MISFORTUNES ARE BEHIND US AND THAT WE CAN FINALLY LIVE THE LIVES OTHERS WOULD HAVE DENIED US.
NOW GATHER OUR THINGS. WE'RE GOING HOME.

YES...YOUR MAJESTY.

IS YOUR LOVE FOR MAAR STRONG, SOLDIER?
AS AN OAK...YOUR MAJESTY.

AND YOUR LOVE FOR ME?

NO NO NOOOO! SHE'S MINE!
NO!
Taake meee...
YOU CAN'T HAVE HER!
...WHAT IN THE GODS?
Taaake meee baaack...
AAGHK--!

Hnnf!
Ooollwynn
GAHK!!
rreleease... meee...
...death magic!
LITTLE ONE...
QUICKLY...

DON'T LISTEN TO HER!
THAT'S THE WITCH SPEAKING, NOT YOUR MOTHER--
AHH!!
Unf!
OLWYN...
MY HEART...
COME BACK TO MEEE...

YESSS...
THE LONELI-NESS...
YOU FEEL IT AS WELL...
TORN FROM EACH OTHER...
TOGETHER AGAIN...
TOGETHER... YES...
CAN YOU HEAR IT?
Isola is calling us hooome...
g-glck... ukk...

Hff
Hff

AAH!
NOOOOOOo
EEEEEE
EEEEeee
nnNAAGH!

M-my face...
...mom said t-take my medicine or--
WAIT...
OH GODS...

I'm... I'm sorry. I don't... I didn't mean to--
I WAS IN ISOLA, I THINK? WITH MY BROTHER AND...
NO, MY SON. ASHER T-TRIED TO PULL ME FROM THE WATER BUT I WAS ALREADY--
I...I... GODSDAMNED I CAN'T THINK WITH THIS SHADOW INSIDE ME!

I FOUND IT. IT'S OLWYN'S BUT...IT WANTED ME. NO ONE'S EVER--
I WOULD GIVE IT BACK, IF I COULD. IF IT WOULD MAKE YOU HAPPY, CAPTAIN.
IF YOU WOULD LOVE ME.

I DON'T KNOW WHAT HAPPENED TO YOU OR WHAT KIND OF CREATURE YOU'VE BECOME, MILUŠE...
I DON'T LOVE YOU.

BUT...YOU COULD.
RIGHT?

YOU WERE A LIAR AND A THIEF BEFORE THE SHADE ENCHANTED YOU.
I WOULD PUT MY KNIFE THROUGH YOUR HEART RIGHT NOW...
...BUT I'M NOT SURE IT WOULDN'T HURT MY QUEEN.

WHAT DO WE DO WITH THIS WITCH, MAJESTY? SHE LOOKS EXACTLY LIKE YOU.
IF SHE'S SPOTTED HERE IN THE WOODS, WORD OF QUEEN OLWYN'S RETURN WILL TRAVEL QUICKLY BACK TO THE KINGDOM.
IT MIGHT STOP MAAR FROM MARCHING TO WAR WITH--

WAIT.

STAND UP STRAIGHT.

YOUR MAJESTY!! WE FOUND YOU!
I MEAN... YOU FOUND US!

SHE WERE TELLIN' THE TRUTH.

HEAR ME, SOLDIERS OF MAAR!

I WILL NOT HAVE YOU MARCH TO WAR WITH PALAGRINE ROCK.
YOUR KINGDOM NEEDS YOU.
BUT...BUT THEY SAID YOU WAS KIDNAPPED, MAJESTY!
THAT KING BASTIAN TOOK YOU AWAY TO THE ROCK.

YOUR QUEEN IS SAFE AND READY TO RETURN TO HER PALACE.
GATHER YOUR THINGS.
WE'RE HEADING HOME!

FIRES ARE OUT.
THEY'RE NEARLY PACKED.
AND THE SCOUTS ARE ALREADY MOVING BACK NORTH...
SHE DID IT.

I JUST HOPE WE HAVEN'T MADE THINGS WORSE.

WE BOUGHT OURSELVES SOME TIME...
...BUT WE NEED TO GET YOU BACK ON THE THRONE BEFORE MILUŠE GETS TOO COMFORTABLE AS QUEEN AND TURNS THE KINGDOM INTO HER OWN--

HALLUM!!

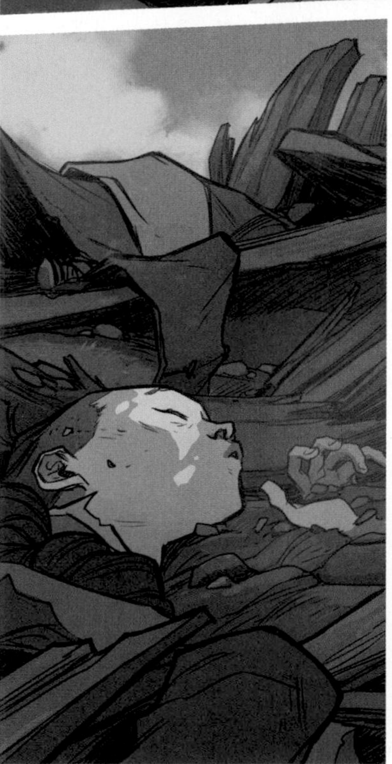

MAY YOUR SOULS FLY TO *ISOLA*.

ALL OF YOU.

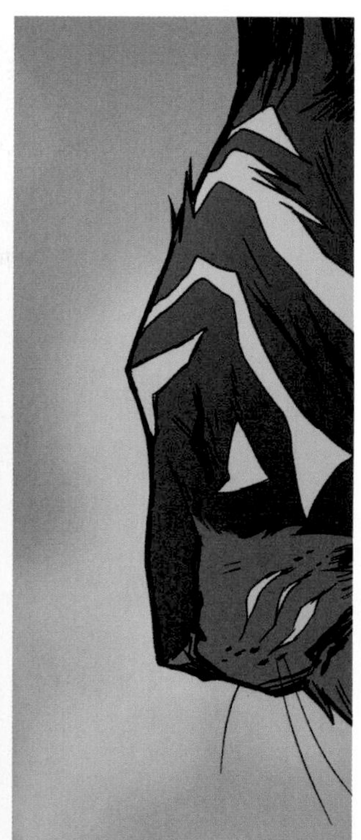

THAT THING INSIDE MILUŠE... IT WAS A PART OF *YOU*. YOU COULD FEEL THAT, RIGHT?
WELL, IT KNEW YOUR SECRETS. *ALL* OF THEM. IT TOLD ME...
I KNOW WHAT YOUR MOTHER DID.
AND I KNOW THAT *YOU'VE* KNOWN ALL ALONG.

ISOLA

COVER GALLERY

Each issue of the ISOLA comic book shipped with two different cover options - the 'A' covers continued to offer Karl Kerschl's unified, graphic presentation of the series' characters as they have since Chapter One, while the variant 'B' covers opened the world up to interpretation by some of the comic industry's most talented artists. Here's a look at all of them.

'A' COVERS - Art by Karl Kerschl

'B' COVERS - Art by Jen Bartel, Sarah Stone, Fiona Staples, Mingjue Helen Chen, and Becky Cloonan

ISSUE 6 - COVER A by Karl Kerschl

ISSUE 6 - COVER B by Jen Bartel

ISSUE 7 - COVER A by Karl Kerschl

ISSUE 7 - COVER B by Sarah Stone

ISSUE 8 - COVER A by Karl Kerschl

ISSUE 8 - COVER B by Fiona Staples

ISSUE 9 - COVER A by Karl Kerschl

ISSUE 9 - COVER B by Mingjue Helen Chen

ISSUE 10 - COVER A by Karl Kerschl

ISSUE 10 - COVER B by Becky Cloonan

ISOLA BEHIND THE SCENES

A MINI-COMIC BY STAFF REPORTER AND COLOURIST
MICHELE ASSARASAKORN

IN ANTICIPATION OF TEAM ISOLA'S TRIP TO TOKYO IN THE FALL OF 2018, MICHELE CREATED A SHORT 'ZINE' CHRONICLING THE CREATION OF THE FIRST VOLUME OF THE SERIES. SHE SUBSEQUENTLY ADDED A MORE DETAILED LOOK AT HER COLOURING PROCESS TO THE INITIAL SHORT. THE FOLLOWING PAGES ARE AN EDITED EXCERPT OF HER 35-PAGE MINI-COMIC.

THE WRITING DEPARTMENT
TIME TO SHOW THEM HOW WE PUT ISOLA TOGETHER, BRENDEN!
DO WE HAVE TO SHOW THEM OUR SCRIPTS?
I'M ASHAMED, KARL.
SUPER OFFICIAL SCRIPT?
ISOLA #1
WE DON'T USE TRADITIONAL SCRIPTS UNTIL LETTERING...
EVERY ISSUE OF ISOLA STARTS AS A SERIES OF NOTES BASED ON OUR CONVERSATIONS. SOMETIMES THOSE NOTES GET BROKEN DOWN IN GREATER DETAIL OR WRITTEN OUT AS COMPLETE SCENES. WE INCLUDE MORE DETAIL IN SOME SCENES THAN OTHERS, WITH FULL SCRIPT OCCASIONALLY REARING ITS HEAD, WHICH ALLOWS KARL
A GREATER UNDERSTANDING OF HOW TO RENDER THE CHARACTERS' "ACTING" ON THE PAGE. FROM THIS POINT, IT'S ALL ON HIM TO INTERPRET NOTES AND SCRIPT INTO ART.
ALL ON ME, Hmm?
NO PRESSURE.
ART!
I USED TO DRAW ALL THIS STUFF ON PAPER BUT NOW EVERYTHING IS DONE JUST ON AN IPAD!
IPAD
APPLE PEN
I USE AN APP CALLED CLIP STUDIO PAINT, WHICH WAS DESIGNED SPECIFICALLY TO MAKE COMICS, AND I REALLY ONLY USE TWO
TOOLS:
: INKED CHARACTERS
6B-PENCIL
: SOFTER BACKGROUNDS
4B-PENCIL
SOMETIMES THERE ARE LOTS OF DIFFERENT LAYERS FOR EVERY PANEL ON THE PAGE IF I'M ADDING A LOT OF EFFECTS AND ATMOSPHERE AND STUFF. TRUST ME - MICHELE LOVES THIS.
MAYBE CUT BACK ON THE LAYERS A BIT...

LAYOUT

I START WITH VERY ROUGH SHAPES THAT NO ONE ELSE CAN MAKE ANY SENSE OF, THEN GRADUALLY REFINE THOSE SHAPES INTO A FINISHED PAGE I'M HAPPY WITH.

SOMETIMES DURING THE PROCESS, I WILL JUST MAKE STUFF UP THAT WASN'T IN OUR SCRIPT AND ADD IT TO THE STORY.

TRUST ME -BRENDEN **LOVES** THIS.

I... KIND OF LOVE THIS?

POKE POKE

ANYWAY, WHEN IT'S ALL DONE I SCRIBBLE A BUNCH OF NOTES TO MICHELE TO POINT OUT THINGS SHE MIGHT NEED TO KNOW, LIKE WHERE THE LIGHT SOURCES MIGHT BE, WHAT TIME OF DAY IT IS IN THE SCENE, WHERE TO ADD MORE FOG OR MOSS.

AND THEN I START THE NEXT PAGE.

AND THEN THE NEXT ONE AFTER THAT.

AND THE NEXT ONE.

THEN THE NEXT ONE...

AND THEN ANOTHER ONE...

AND ANOTHER..

AND YUP, ANOTHER...

AND ANOTHER..

ANOTHER..

ON TO... COLOURING

I USUALLY HIRE SOMEONE FOR THIS, AS IT CAN BE TIME CONSUMING.

WITH THE FLATS, I GO IN AND READJUST COLOURS TO FIT THEM INTO THE TIME OF DAY/ENVIRONMENT THEY'RE IN. IT CAN BE HARD TO PICK SO THIS IS WHERE THE STORY TELLING COMES IN.

FOR EXAMPLE, THE TEMPERATURE OF THE PALETTE CAN HAVE A VERY DIFFERENT IMPACT ON A SCENE.

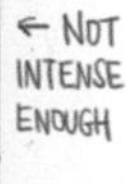

AND WITH THE DRAWINGS FINALIZED, THE SCRIPT CAN BE COMPLETED AND SENT TO ADITYA FOR LETTERING.

LETTERING + FX

FEATURING

ADITYA BIDIKAR

BASED ON DISCUSSIONS WITH KARL AND BRENDEN, I DECIDED TO LOOK AT THE LETTERING IN ISOLA AS IF I WAS LETTERING A TRANSLATED COMIC THAT WAS ORIGINALLY MADE IN AN ALIEN LANGUAGE, AND TRIED TO COME UP WITH A STYLE THAT REFLECTED THAT.

A HUGE REFERENCE POINT FOR ME HERE IS THE SOUND EFFECTS KARL DRAWS ALL THOSE AFTER I'VE DONE A FIRST DRAFT OF THE LETTERING.

THESE SOUNDS GIVE ME A HINT OF THE WORLD OF ISOLA, AND I TRY AND STAY TRUE TO THAT WORLD - WHICH IS WHY I (DIGITALLY) HAND-DRAW ALL THE BALLOONS AND THE SHOUTS COMING FROM PEOPLE, AND EVEN THE SCRIPT I ENDED UP CREATING FOR THE MORO FROM ISSUE 3 ON.

NOBODY ELSE ON TEAM ISOLA KNOWS HOW THE MORO SCRIPT WORKS. THEY SEND ME THE DIALOGUE AND THEY JUST HAVE TO TRUST I'M NOT PUTTING IN ANY RUDE WORDS.

ONCE THE FILES ARE SENT TO PRINT, THERE'S NOTHING LEFT TO DO BUT WAIT FOR THE NEW ISSUE OF ISOLA TO SHIP TO COMIC STORES ALL OVER THE WORLD.

THANKS FOR READING!

THIS PROJECT HAS BEEN A LABOUR OF LOVE SINCE ITS INCEPTION. WE HOPE YOU ENJOYED THE GRAPHIC NOVEL AND THIS BRIEF LOOK BEHIND THE SCENES AT HOW WE PUT IT ALL TOGETHER.

STUDIO LOUNAK, MONTREAL 2018

ADITYA B.

FOR A MORE IN-DEPTH LOOK AT HOW ISOLA IS MADE, INCLUDING DETAILED COLOUR AND PHOTOSHOP TECHNIQUES, CHECK OUT MICHELE'S 35-PAGE ZINE ON THE SUBJECT, AVAILABLE ONLINE NOW AT MSASSYK.COM

BRENDEN FLETCHER is a *New York Times* bestselling writer of comics and cartoons. He's known for his work on DC Comics' titles *Batgirl, Black Canary* and *Gotham Academy* (with Karl Kerschl and MSassyK), his acclaimed Image Comics series MOTOR CRUSH (with Aditya Bidikar) and various other illustrated/animated bits and bobs in books and TV. He lives in Brooklyn, NY, with his wife and cat.

KARL KERSCHL draws comics all day long and has been doing so ever since Brenden Fletcher talked him into it in high school. Since then he has worked on a number of titles for Marvel and DC Comics including *Superman, The Flash, Deadpool, Spider-Man, Teen Titans*, *Wonder Woman* and the acclaimed YA series *Gotham Academy*.
His ongoing webcomic, *The Abominable Charles Christopher*, won the Eisner Award for Best Webcomic in 2011.
He lives in Montréal, Canada, surrounded at all times by his children and imported Japanese robot toys.

MSASSYK (MICHELE ASSARASAKORN) is a freelance artist in various industries but is primarily known as colourist on titles like *Gotham Academy, Critical Role Vox Machina Origins*, *Ms. Marvel Annual*, and the *Wonder Woman 75th Anniversary* special.
She is currently drawing a YA (young adult) comic and spends the rest of her time playing outside in Vancouver, Canada.

ADITYA BIDIKAR is the award-winning letterer for *The White Trees, VS* and *Little Bird* for Image Comics, *Hellblazer* for DC Comics, and *These Savage Shores* and *Deep Roots* for Vault Comics, among others.

He lives and works out of Pune, India, with a cat called Loki for company.